A N~~~~
Christmas
In Florida

Sue Carabine
with Rochelle Lynn Holt

Illustrations by
Shauna Mooney Kawasaki

GIBBS·SMITH
P
PUBLISHER

SALT LAKE CITY

04 03   6 5 4

Copyright © 1999 by Gibbs Smith, Publisher

Book design by Mary Ellen Thompson,
TTA Design
Printed in China

Published by
Gibbs Smith, Publisher
P.O. Box 667
Layton, Utah 84041

Orders: (1-800) 748-5439
E-mail: info@gibbs-smith.com
Website: www.gibbs-smith.com

ISBN 0-87905-928-1

'Twas the night before Christmas
in Florida State,
The snowbirds were coming
'cause they couldn't wait.

They'd shed winter woolies
they wore while up north,
Donned T-shirts and sandals
and Bermuda shorts!

Fishing poles, golf clubs,
and swimsuits galore
They carried with gusto,
while some guys yelled, "Fore!"

The tourists were baking
bare flesh on the beaches,
While nibbling on oranges,
grapefruit, and peaches.

They spied leaping dolphins
and searched for seashells,
Then returned to their condos,
RVs, and motels.

Their cameras were clicking
at each thing in sight
All through the day,
and also at night.

Some had forgotten
St. Nick was due soon,
Then a child pointed skyward
around about noon.

A small plane was writing
some words in the sky,
And all who could read it
heaved a great sigh.

For it said, "Dear old Santa,
he may be delayed
On his journey worldwide
in time for Christmas Day."

Some parents were troubled,
most kids worried sick,
He'd not failed them before,
their dear old St. Nick.

The rumors began,
"Where on earth can he be?
Perhaps on the Cape,
maybe down in the Keys?"

But everyone knows
of this state's fun attractions,
Maybe Santa and friends
got caught up in the action.

Well, believe it or not,
that was just what occurred;
He'd come early to Florida
because he had heard

That this was the place
if you're tired or worn out
The folks here are jolly,
they'll not let you pout!

So he made his first stop
in Boca Raton,
He was massaged at a spa
right down to the bone!

The elves and the reindeer
got "the works" too,
Even Rudolph's red nose
was polished on cue!

St. Augustine's Fountain of Youth
was up next,
Where Nick showed off
biceps, triceps and pecs.

He got so excited
as he dropped by Epcot,
'Cause a stranger to all
of these countries he's not.

Santa couldn't recall
when he'd had so much fun
As the hours he'd spent
in the Magic Kingdom.

He wore a disguise
and dressed incognito,
And tried hard to control
his loud Ho! Ho! Ho!

To do this was hard
as he heard girls and boys,
Their laughs and their giggles—
he shared all of their joys.

He had so much fun
he repeated the rides,
Screaming and yelling,
about splitting his sides!

Then on to the race track,
Hialeah by name,
Santa found that his reindeer
he had to restrain.

They knew they could beat
every horse on the track;
It took all of his strength
to hold them all back.

It was right after this that
St. Nick stopped to see
What the great folks were doing
in Tallahassee.

Then as he swooped down,
he frowned in dismay
As none of the children
were outside at play.

He peeked in some windows
and saw to his horror
That most of his kids
had their heads bowed in sorrow.

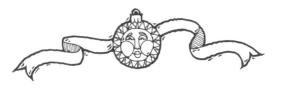

What could be wrong
and why are they so sad?
He knew they were good kids,
not one of them bad.

He discovered the answer
by watching TV
For he saw there HIS picture
as plain as could be,

And then heard the announcement
of Governor Bush
That Kris Kringle was tardy.
He 'bout fell on his tush!

Time had flown by
since he came to this state,
Maybe this night before Christmas
he'd be very late.

In fact, some of his children
would think him a fake
Unless Santa was helped
by the guys at the Cape.

Well, Canaveral came through
and they lent him the shuttle;
The reindeer were jealous
but had no rebuttal.

So Santa Claus transferred
his huge precious cargo
And guided the rocket ship
down toward Key Largo.

As he climbed down a chimney
at a staggering rate,
Not planning to eat
what he usually ate,

He found on the hearth
no cookies this year,
But a rich key lime pie
and a glass of good cheer!

Then a family in Naples,
just outside of town,
Left Santa some grits and
a plate of hash browns.

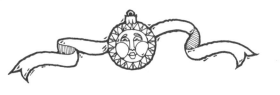

"This state of Florida
is my kind of place,"
Said Nick to himself
as he ate in great haste.

He flew over hibiscus
and swaying palm trees,
Noting the beauty
of Lake Okeechobee.

At the dark Everglades
with its crocs and its gators,
Nick declined to go in there,
even with waders.

He had gifts for the snorklers
and a surfer named Ben.
Santa knew what they'd love
'cause he'd learned to "hang ten."

At Miami Beach
he'd won trophy and cup,
'Cause his voice was the loudest
when he bellowed "SURF'S UP!"

The shuttle took him from
Pensacola to Tampa
And everyone heard it,
even Grandma and Grandpa!

The folks at Daytona
slowed down on the track,
They'd never seen anything
move faster than that!

Finally, jolly old St. Nick
was through,
All gifts were delivered
from the States to Peru.

He decided the shuttle
was so cool to handle,
But still, to his reindeer
it could not hold a candle!

Nevertheless, he was
grateful and proud
And his thanks to the Cape guys
he shouted out loud,

"Without you, this Christmas
might never have come.
Now my kids the world over
will have lots of fun!"

"Thanks for the memories,
dear Florida," said Nick,
"When I need more R & R,
it's you that I'll pick!"

Then his reindeer flew up,
while St. Nick hung on tight
And yelled, "Cheers, Sunshine State,
to you all a good night!"